To Eleanor Berden

John Leatherman
3/31/91

Happy Easter! Enjoy this book!

D.v. Berden,

It was such fun doing this book with John. He is an outstanding young man, and I know you are proud of him, too!

Charleen Brinkley

Jonah
and the
Glass
Mountain

Jonah and the Glass Mountain

Charleen Lewis Brinkley

Illustrated by John Donald Leatherman

VANTAGE PRESS
New York • Los Angeles

To
my beloved children,
John Wayne Brinkley (my pride and joy)
and
Kathleen Brinkley (my answered prayer)

Jonah and the Glass Mountain

CHAPTER ONE

Once upon a time, in a faraway land, lived a lovely princess, Julietta, in a beautiful golden castle. So well loved was she by the king and queen of this fair land that she was never allowed to venture forth out of the palace doors without her faithful nurse.

For on one side of the castle was a huge, ugly, black mountain. And on the other side of the castle was a crystal clear, glass mountain that could be seen for miles and miles around.

Inside the glass mountain lived a complete little village of tiny people, who always seemed to be busy at work. No one had ever seen the tiny people come out, and no one in the village had ever been able to enter the shimmering mass of glass.

The only entrance was at the very top of the glass mountain, and no one had ever tried to climb its slippery surface.

But the little people in the glass mountain were always watching and waiting for a chance to kidnap the little princess, so that she could be their queen and rule their kingdom.

One day—as the princess was playing out in the palace gardens—she became so thirsty, she begged her nurse to please leave her for only a moment and bring her a glass of water.

As the nurse vanished from sight, a secret door in the glass mountain flew open and a parade of tiny soldiers armed with bows, arrows, and little ropes came rushing out. The arrows were so small that the little princess thought mosquitoes were biting her, and she jumped up and down, rubbing her legs, as the arrows pierced her flesh.

They wound their tiny threadlike ropes around and around her until she was bound tightly. Then they lifted her carefully and carried her inside the glass mountain. The secret entrance then closed behind them and sealed itself forever.

She was placed upon their royal throne, clothed in a velvet cloak, and all sorts of good things to eat were bestowed upon her: ice cream, cake, peppermint sticks and gum drops,

gingerbread cookies and candy-coated apples on a stick. A crown of jewels was placed upon her head, and all the subjects of the kingdom bowed down before her. This was not her kingdom, however, and tears streamed down her face as she thought about being their captive and never returning home.

Meanwhile, the nurse returned to the palace gardens to find the princess gone. When the guards could not find her, the nurse rushed into the palace and told the king and queen.

Frantically, they, too, took up the search. And before very long, the people in the town looked toward the glass mountain—only to see their precious little princess sitting sadly upon the velvet throne of the little people, imprisoned in a castle of glass forever.

The king and queen became so filled with grief that a decree was sent out into all the land, stating that anyone who could climb to the top of the glass mountain and rescue the little princess could have her hand in marriage and half the kingdom.

Soon the village was flooded with knights and their beautiful horses from all over the world, and one by one they tried to climb the glass mountain, only to fail time after time.

It seemed impossible, and soon, no one came to even try anymore, and the little town, which had once been so happy, was now quiet and all the people went around with long faces.

Now not far from the castle, there was a boy named Jonah, who took care of his poor widowed mother and farmed their small plot of land with his horse, Hildegarde. Hildegarde was a very special horse, in that he could talk and was most beautiful.

One sunny afternoon, as they were working in the fields, Jonah said, "Hildegarde, wouldn't it be wonderful if we could rescue the little princess?"

And Hildegarde said, "Well, we can, Master Jonah. I'll tell you what to do. Every day, for three weeks, you rub and rub and rub my hair with meal. At the end of the third week, my coat of hair will fairly dazzle the eyesight, and we'll be ready to be on our journey to the township of the Glass Mountain."

So Jonah did just as Hildegarde told him. Every day for three weeks, he rubbed and rubbed Hildegarde's hair until it shone like a mirror. And at the end of the third week, they were ready to ride to the palace and ascend to the top of the glass mountain.

The king and queen were so happy to see Jonah and Hildegarde, because by this time, no one ever came to try and ascend to the top of the glass mountain anymore. A big feast was prepared to celebrate their coming. Hildegarde ate the finest oats in the stable that night.

Very early the next morning, Jonah and Hildegarde were ready to try and climb to the top of the glass mountain, where there was a trap door right above the throne upon which the princess sat.

The whole town turned out to watch them. The people were laughing and clapping and shouting with joy and hope. But everything grew very still and quiet, as Jonah and Hildegarde started the climb. Clippty-clop, clippity-clop, clippity-clop—up they went, only to get almost halfway up and slip back down.

Tears came into Jonah's eyes, but Hildegarde said, "Master Jonah, you try me one more time!"

So up they started again—Clippity-clop, clippity-clop, clippity-clop, clippity-clop—and this time, they got a little more than halfway before they slipped back down once again. Poor little Jonah really broke down this time and cried and cried and cried.

"We can't do it, Hildegarde," said Jonah.

But Hildegarde answered, "Master Jonah, you try me one more time."

Tearfully, Jonah climbed up on Hildegarde to try again—Clippity-clop, clippity-clop, clippity-clop, clippity-clop, clippity-clop—and to the very top they went.

Hildegarde then lifted up his great big hoof and let it slam down upon the trap door, shattering it into a million pieces.

At the sound of the trap door breaking, Julietta looked up to see Jonah on his magnificent horse, and the two of them fell instantly in love.

The little princess stretched out her arms, and Jonah bent down and lifted her up on top of Hildegarde with him. They then rode down the glass mountain where they were met with cheers and hugs and kisses from the king and queen and all the people.

CHAPTER TWO

The king and queen declared a royal holiday, and there was laughter and feasting throughout the whole land. At the end of the week, Jonah and Julietta went before the king and queen and reminded them of the promise they had made. But the king really did not want a commoner like Jonah marrying his daughter. So he schemed to rid himself of Jonah.

"Jonah," said the king, "I'll tell you what I'll do. We'll play a little game of hide-and-seek. First, I'll have Julietta's godmother hide her, and you will look for her. Then we'll let your fairy godmother hide you and see if the little princess can find you. If you can find each other, then I'll let you have her hand in marriage."

So the little princess's fairy godmother hid her in a hot-air balloon sailing across the kingdom. Jonah began looking for her. He looked and looked and looked. He could find her nowhere. Sadly, he walked out into the stables where Hildegarde was busy eating some oats.

"Hildegarde, I guess we are going to have to give up. I can't find the little princess anywhere," said Jonah.

"Well, Master Jonah," Hildegarde replied, "you look up at that hot-air balloon." When Jonah gazed up at the balloon, he saw Julietta in the basket. He shouted for glee because he had found the princess.

Suddenly, the hot-air balloon began descending rapidly toward the surface of the kingdom. It was being pulled by some mysterious suction. Jonah jumped on Hildegarde's back, and they began riding as fast as they could toward where the balloon seemed to be heading. As they breathlessly arrived on that spot, they watched the balloon disappear into the mouth of a dark, forbidding cave. Following Julietta's screams for help, Hildegarde galloped into the bowels of the cave.

Hildegarde and Jonah followed a path in the dim light of the cave. All around them strange creatures lurked in the shadows and hollows along the path.

All of a sudden, four gigantic eyes emerged slowly from a clump of weeds beneath a towering waterfall. The creature that appeared was unlike any that Jonah and Hildegarde had ever seen. He had two heads with huge nostrils. Every few moments he would sniff the weeds around him, and both heads would sneeze with such force that tornadolike winds would rock the cavern. He tried to cover his mouths, but his four legs were too short. Jonah quickly realized that the monster's sneezing had created the suction.

High above the water, Julietta was clinging for dear life to the basket, dangling precariously from a ledge. Every time the monster sneezed, the winds would rattle her back and forth like a windchime.

"He must be allergic to the weeds," said Hildegarde. "I will stop his sneezing." Hildegarde gobbled down most of the weeds in front of him. The next time the creature sniffed the air, he stopped, and two large smiles spread across his faces.

His two heads began to speak in perfect harmony. "Thank you for removing those awful weeds. I am a Bronchitisaurus, and I love to smell wild flowers. However, when I sniffed

those weeds, I began sneezing so harshly I couldn't stop."

"We were glad we could help you," Jonah replied. "We are from another kingdom outside your cave many miles away. The girl on the ledge is the princess of our kingdom. We have come to take her back to our kingdom. Soon, I will marry the princess, and you and all your friends are invited to come to the wedding. There will be a great celebration, and each of you will be greeted warmly."

Bronchitisaurus was delighted to accept Jonah's invitation. For years he had wondered if there was life outside his cave.

Jonah and Hildegarde got into the basket beneath the hot-air balloon. As they did, Hildegarde instructed Bronchitisaurus to sniff the few remaining weeds one more time and to direct his sneezing toward the balloon. He sneezed his most powerful sneezes ever. The balloon was blown swiftly out of the cave up through the atmosphere and floated down safely in front of the castle.

CHAPTER THREE

Now, it was Jonah's turn, and his fairy godmother took him to the faraway land called, "Forever Halloween." Those who live in "Forever Halloween Land" are forever the characters they choose to be on Halloween each year.

The little Princess began her search throughout the kingdom but couldn't find Jonah anywhere. So, like Jonah, she sought Hildegarde's counsel in the stables.

Hildegarde told her to mount him and hold on tightly, as they were going to ride for a long time. Sure enough, it was twilight by the time they reached "Forever Halloween Land."

Hildegarde said, "Princess, you will find Jonah inside this land."

The princess began her search wandering down long, dark paths and up and down valleys and hills filled with spooks and goblins of every description. With every step, she kept in mind

this was only a make-believe land. Each Halloween is always filled with sinister monsters, but they are only disguises for ordinary people caught up in the fun of the season. Those that inhabitated "Forever Halloween Land" just never took off their disguises. Julietta concentrated and thought, *Jonah must have planned some kind of clues for me to find him.*

Hildegarde, sensing her discouragement, trotted up beside her and led her to a beautiful field with a strange elephantlike creature sitting in a clump of weeds next to a waterfall. Then he began to sniff the weeds around him and sneeze ferociously. Julietta realized it had to be Jonah. He knew that she would remember Bronchitisaurus. Quickly, she mounted Hildegarde and rode as fast as she could toward the creature shouting, "Jonah, Jonah!"

She had found him. Jonah's fairy godmother appeared and transformed the creature back to Jonah. His fairy godmother then transported them back to their kingdom as quickly as possible.

CHAPTER FOUR

Jonah was certain now that the king and queen would let him marry the little princess, but the king craftily said, "Jonah, I just can't bear to think of you and the princess getting married and living in the castle and having to look at that big, old, ugly black mountain that has been next to the castle all these years. I'll tell you what I'll do: if you can get rid of that black mountain, I'll let you marry the little princess."

Jonah didn't know what he was going to do. He went out to the stable and told Hildegarde his problem.

Hildegarde thought a minute and said, "Master Jonah, you take me over to the blacksmith's shop and have him make me the biggest, heaviest horseshoes he has ever made and put them on me."

So Jonah did! The blacksmith in the village made Hildegarde the heaviest horseshoes in the land and put them on his hoofs. Then Hildegarde and Jonah set out for the black mountain.

When they got there, Hildegarde told Jonah, "You get up in the saddle, and you ride me around and around and around this mountain. And every time we go around, we will trample down the mountain—just a little bit at a time."

And sure enough, with every circle of the mountain they made, it slowly began to flatten until soon it was as flat as a pancake. The king was amazed and furious. Jonah had outsmarted him again!

No one had ever seen on the other side of the black mountain, and much to everyone's surprise and delight, there was a beautiful green forest with small lakes and wild animals running all about—it was indeed a beautiful sight for all to behold.

Surely now, the king would let Jonah and the little princess marry. But the king had thought of an even worse challenge for Jonah.

He told Jonah, "There is only one more thing that I must demand of you. Hildegarde is the most beautiful horse in the kingdom. You and the princess can never go out riding together because there is not a single horse to match Hildegarde's beauty in the whole kingdom. So, if you can find another horse as magnificent as Hildegarde, I promise you, I will not hesitate in letting you have the princess's hand in marriage."

Jonah felt that he had been beaten for sure this time.

There couldn't possibly be another horse—anywhere—like Hildegarde.

But to his surprise, Hildegarde said, "Master Jonah, there is a female horse exactly like me. Her name is Heather. She lives in a valley guarded by a wild, mean, fire-breathing stallion on the other side of the world. No one has ever journeyed there before! I'll tell you what we'll do.

"First, you get us a big barrel of seed and a big barrel of meat. Then, you get a strong rope," Hildegarde continued.

So Jonah got the barrel of seed, the barrel of meat, and the rope. Then, he and Hildegarde were ready to start on their journey for the wild horses' valley on the other side of the world.

After they had been traveling for days and days and days, huge flocks of birds filled the skies. They chirped and cawed angrily at Hildegarde and Jonah.

Jonah said, "Hildegarde, I believe all the birds in the world are attacking us."

Hildegarde replied, "Well, they are! You get down and empty the barrel of seeds we brought with us, and while they are eating the seeds, we'll ride off and leave them."

So Jonah got down quickly and emptied the barrel of seeds and while the birds were eating them, he and Hildegarde rode off and left them.

It wasn't long before they entered some dense, dark jungles, and suddenly wild animals of all sorts were running after them.

And Jonah said, "Hildegarde, I believe all the animals in the world are chasing us."

And Hildegarde answered, "Well, they are! Get down and empty the barrel of meat, and while they are eating it, we will ride away and leave them."

So Jonah got off Hildegard and emptied the barrel of meat, and sure enough, while all the animals of the jungle gnawed on the meat, he and Hildegarde ran off and left them far behind.

Jonah and Hildegarde finally found Heather in a beautiful, peaceful valley hidden in a forest. As Hildegarde had said, she was guarded by a ferocious, fire-breathing stallion running wildly about.

"Now, Jonah," Hildegarde said, "when you lasso that stallion with the rope we brought, he will be as tame as can be, and he will let us take Heather."

Jonah protested, "I could never lasso such a fast horse."

Hildegarde replied, "I will chase him around the valley and tire him out. Then you will be able to lasso him without any problem."

As Hildegarde approached Heather, however, he fell instantly in love with her and Heather with him. Overwhelmed with adoration, Hildegarde forgot about his plan. The two love-struck horses gazed dreamily into each other's eyes and rubbed noses.

Meanwhile though, the stallion exploded in anger and charged fiercely toward Hildegarde.

Jonah shouted hysterically, "Hildegarde, the stallion is charging. He is going to kill you."

Hildegarde, still entranced with love, did not move. Jonah suddenly realized he had to be the hero this time. Observing that the weeds in the field were just like the ones in

Bronchitisaurus's cave, he plucked a handful and bravely strode between Hildegarde and the stallion. He sniffed the weeds. Then, he turned toward the stallion and sneezed with galelike force. The sneeze propelled the stallion against a huge rock, where he collapsed. Jonah then threw the lasso effortlessly around his neck.

When the stallion regained consciousness, he was as tame as could be and quietly slipped away.

The danger passed, Hildegarde declared, "Jonah, we can go home now."

Upon their return to the kingdom, the king and queen, astounded by the beauty of Hildegarde and Heather together, finally gave up and let Jonah and Julietta marry.

The entire kingdom took part in the wedding celebrations. Bronchitisaurus and his cave-dwelling friends were there. Many of the characters from "Forever Halloween Land" even came.

After many days of merriment, Jonah and the princess settled themselves in the palace where they lived happily ever after.

As for Hildegarde and Heather, they spent the rest of their days in the royal stables and running free in the "Kingdom of Sumware."